Manners Matter

Good Manners at the Library

Gloria Santos

illustrated by
Lorna William

PowerKiDS
press.

New York

Published in 2018 by The Rosen Publishing Group, Inc.
29 East 21st Street, New York, NY 10010

First Edition

Managing Director: Nathalie Beullens-Maoui
Editor, English: Melissa Raé Shofner
Book Design: Raúl Rodriguez
Illustrator: Lorna William

Cataloging-in-Publication Data

Names: Santos, Gloria.
Title: Good manners at the library / Gloria Santos.
Description: New York : PowerKids Press, 2018. | Series: Manners matter | Includes index.
Identifiers: ISBN 9781538320785 (pbk.) | ISBN 9781508157281 (library bound) | ISBN 9781538320280 (6 pack)
Subjects: LCSH: Etiquette for children and teenagers–Juvenile fiction. | Libraries–Juvenile fiction.
Classification: LCC PZ7.S26 Goo 2018 | DDC [E]–dc23

Manufactured in the United States of America

CPSIA Compliance Information: Batch #BS17PK: For further information contact Rosen Publishing, New York, New York at 1-800-237-9932

Contents

The library is a great place.
I go there with my friend Tara.

I like to read books about dinosaurs.

Tara wants to learn about sports.

Tara asks the librarian where the soccer books are.

8

She thanks him for his help.

We take turns
reading out loud.

We use our inside voices.

When we're done reading,
we put away our books.

Sometimes there are crafts at the library.
Today we make bookmarks.

"May I please use the crayons?"

Tara covers her mouth to sneeze.
"Achoo!" "Bless you," everyone says.

The librarian gives
Tara a tissue.

15

I sign up to use a computer.

Everyone gets twenty minutes.

It's good to share.

I push in my chair and look for Tara.

Tara is looking at
books again.

Tara finds ten books about basketball
and ten books about swimming.

She brings them to the librarian.
"Excuse me," she says.

I help Tara carry her library books.
Tara's mom holds the door open.

We can't wait to visit
the library again!

23

Words to Know

computer

crayons

dinosaur

Index

24